# MAX ABADDON AND THE GHOST AND THE GRAVE

A MAX ABADDON SHORT STORY.
BOOK 2.5 IN THE
MAX ABADDON SERIES

Justin S. Leslie

Paperback ISBN: 978-1-7353035-7-4
E-book ISBN: 978-1-7353035-6-7

Contact Information
Email: Abaddonbooks@hotmail.com
Facebook: @Maxabaddonbooks
Website: www.JustinLeslie.com

*"I am prepared to meet my Maker. Whether my Maker is prepared for the ordeal of meeting me is another matter."*

—WINSTON CHURCHILL

# NOTE FROM THE AUTHOR

Here we find Max settling in with the realities of the world around him, becoming more relaxed with the Magical and Ethereal communities. The Balance has occurred, and the regular world is now aware that everything that goes bump in the night, for the most part, is real. In this short story, Max, well . . . Max is about to learn a valuable lesson about making bets at the bar with a stranger.

Fate has handed Max something that will affect not only his, but the lives of his friends. Only time will tell.
We also meet two new characters that have a rather sorted future in the series. Anyone like pirates and ghosts? There may be a cameo. The Fallen Angel has several ways in from multiple Planes, but only one way out.

Sit back, have a drink, and enjoy the ride.

# CHAPTER 1

"Max, can you get that thing to calm down?" Phil said, flooring the accelerator of the Black Beast. The engine growled under the stress of the large boot asking for all the power the machine had to offer.

"Trying. I think it just tried to eat my...,omph," I let out, landing on my back in the bed of the truck.

Phil and I had made the mistake of helping out an old friend instead of going on an all-night bender. Regrets, I have a few...

The creature we'd agreed to catch was a rather lively Fiend Hound terrorizing a local beach. Almost identical to the ones we'd encountered in Carvels Manor a few months back.

Coincidentally, we'd kept one of those hounds and given it to Davros, a rather old Vampire that sat on the Supreme Council. Once he'd heard of another one being let loose from the Plane, he just "had to have it."

Shaped like a dog, with armor resembling that of a turtle, the creature's massive teeth protruded from jaws sitting below two black oval eyes. It was all topped off with a tail that could turn one's guts into spaghetti.

"Nah, bruther, I think it's trying to make friends with your leg," Phil bellowed, laughing out loud.

While the creatures looked like nightmare fuel, they did have a rather passionate side. Highly illegal, and one of only two

I was aware of, we needed to get it off the streets before it caused a scene. Normal folks might not take well to a hellhound running around and all.

The plan had been simple. Go find it (easy part), pick it up (easy part two), and drive it back to the Atheneum. The not-easy part.

I reached down, trying to put the leather rope around its overly wide neck. "Alright, fella, last time. I'm not asking nic—" Again, the beast lurched over, flipping me on my back.

It stood over me, maw open, slime running down its fangs and landing perfectly on my face. The hound's breath was a mix of decay and the ocean. I was guessing it spent most of its day drinking seawater.

I gagged and lifted my finger, pointing a spark of hellfire directly at it, its bottomless black eyes reflecting the blood-red flame. The creature backed up, sitting down in the bed of the truck, lowering its head like a dog that was about to get smacked with a newspaper for peeing on the rug.

"Got him," I yelled as the smell of Phil lighting a cigarette filled the air.

I heard him chuckle as I leaned on the tailgate of the truck, wiping my face off and taking a breath of fresh, humid Florida air.

***

After hearing Phil tell the humiliating story of how the evening had gone wrong on the way back, Davros nodded his head, turning to leave. Before he did, though, he stopped, looking back at me.

"Max," the smooth yet authoritative voice came oozing from Davros. "Here, for your troubles." Davros flipped a gold coin in my direction, with me barely catching it. "Drinks on me tonight."

We watched as the Old Vampire walked out the door petting the animal on the head. I could swear he was again making kissy noises at the hound.

"Bruther, you're on your own tonight," Phil chuffed. "It's late, and I have to run a job in the morning."

I smirked at Phil. This was the first time in forever he was passing on a night of drinking. "You alright?"

"I'm tired, and I promised Jenny I'd be up in the morning." Phil looked suddenly exhausted.

"Get some rest. I'm heading over to the Fallen Angel. Two drinks, Scout's honor."

"Save some gas for tomorrow night. I have more snake oil coming in this week."

As we liked to call it, Phil's magic snake oil was a cure for all that ailed you. Especially hangovers.

After our encounter with Lilith last year, Petro—my trusted Pixie companion who just happened to be on his honeymoon—and I had decided to move out on our own. Plus, with Tom back, things had started getting crowded around the Atheneum.

Trish, the owner of the Fallen Angel, just happened to own the building where the old Transitions Office used to be before it was shut down. Upstairs was a full two-bedroom apartment. Which, again, just happened to be next door to FA's.

"Maybe. I think Kim might actually go on a date with me tomorrow. Tell everyone I said hello."

I walked down to the Postern, gating to my apartment. The Postern was a room with ten gates. To date, I had only worked out three of them. On the other hand, Tom had figured out two others only to basically lose the keys to them. The Postern was everywhere and nowhere all at the same time.

The interesting thing about the move had been its simplicity. Tom had given over most of the furniture once he was no longer presumed dead, including King Arthur's supposed desk. Still didn't believe that one; it wasn't round. He had moved back into his old house, only to leave again on some type of job for the council.

When I had moved to my new apartment, Devin had mysteriously gifted me a door that took me directly into the room just as it had been at the Atheneum. The funny thing was, I could still decide where to walk out of that door: my apartment or the old facility.

Making things even more confusing, Devin—whom I was sure was the Devil—had also gifted me Tom's old lab and bar. I was pretty sure Tom had had no say in the matter. Family, what can I say?

The Postern and lab below the office had, in fact, just moved with me. I had spent countless days trying to figure out the math behind it fitting between the first and second floors, giving up after a long night of drilling through the floor after Petro and I had dusted off a fifth of rum.

Much like FA's, it was simple. Find two locations in the apartment and bind the gates together. Wanted to get to the Postern? Just open the closet. Need to get to the lab? Go through the door under the stairs. While Tom made it appear like some type of Gate magic, I knew Devin was somehow involved. Ying Sue had even come by with a housewarming gift and had been surprised by the gate work. I, of course, kept the source a secret. Still, I believed she knew.

FA's was similar. Its primary location was in St. Augustine, Florida. However, you could get there from several other storefronts in various cities. Since the Balance, though, that had slightly changed. No regulars allowed, meaning nonmagical types. Open the door, pass the ward, and there you are. Trish had suggested that there were doors in other places, but had never expanded.

Walking through the door, the smell of burnt butter and steak mixed together with the tang of copper from the rustic roof, formed a grin on my face.

"Trish, nice crowd tonight," I said, walking up to the bar pulling out a seat, taking a minute to ensure I had gotten all the mess off me earlier.

A man sitting at the other side of the bar looked up. He was wearing a long black trench coat, sported lengthy hair, and an almost longer reddish beard. The guy looked scary. His trench coat was scarred and tired looking from years of abuse, and God knows what else. His eyes glowed for a second as he stood up and walked out. The man to my other side, looked at him with a familiar gaze.

"Ya, it's been interesting, to say the least. A few new faces tonight," Trish said, smiling.

As always, she knew just what to hand me. A Vamp Amber, made in Romania by one of the most renowned Vs on earth, Anna Vlad. Her brother, on the other hand...

I took a pull, letting the night's excitement drain away. "Ahh," I let out, slapping the gold coin on the bar top. "Think this will cover it?"

Trish looked at the coin, cocking her head slightly. She was getting something from it. I was pretty sure Trish was some type of goddess. "I think you can buy all the drinks you want with that," she exhaled as the man sitting next to me leaned over.

"Nice coin," the low, rustic yet precise voice said.

"Thanks, just got it. Not really sure what it is," I said, not caring that the coin had been sitting on the bar before I put it between my teeth, biting it like they did in the old movies.

The man was dressed in a black outfit, with a long coat that flowed almost like a cape and a hood pulled up over his head. The peak of his nose and some tendrils of hair protruded out, his eyes glowing slightly. In most normal places, this would seem odd. Not at FA's.

"Tell you what, friend. What do you say we grab a table and play a little game? I win, you can either give me that coin or run an errand for me. You win, I'll give you this."

The odd man pulled out a silver version of the exact same coin, slapping it on the bar top and again getting Trish's attention. I hadn't seen that expression on her face before.

I finished the rest of my beer in one pull, letting out a belch. "Tell you what; you get the next round of drinks, I'm in."

We stood up, walking over to one of the far tables in the corner. Trish had a few games on the shelf by the fireplace. These weren't cheesy board games, though. Chess- and checkerboards made out of pure silver, older than the games themselves, gleamed on the shelf, more for show than anything else. Tonight, however, they would get a workout.

Trish looked at me, grimacing slightly. I think she wanted the coins.

"No Monopoly, I take it?" I said, breaking the silence from the walkover. The man was taller than I'd expected, and stood up with an odd posture. Not too straight, but more than average. The gait of his walk was slightly off, as if his arms and legs were not moving in sync.

The man didn't respond, only grabbed a solid oak case off the shelf. We both sat down. Trish came over with two more drinks, again giving the man a strange look. Not one to signal me but one of slight confusion. She was trying to figure out who or, for that matter, *what* this person was.

Push came to shove, Amon—the ever-hidden cook in the kitchen—would be there to end the world or something like that.

"Thank you," the man said in a polite, old-fashioned manner to Trish as she walked off.

"Chess. It's been a while," I said, breaking the ice. It was starting to get awkward, and I considered the option of just walking away.

To hell with it. I only had a ten-foot walk, and this was the first mildly interesting person I had met in some time that wasn't trying to have me killed. At least, I hoped not.

"I like this place. It reminds me of home," the man said, pulling the cloak off his head, revealing a full head of immaculately straight hair. He had a serious face, and also one that was not from here, I reflected, trying to pinpoint what he was.

Much like a craft—one of those human husks driven by a Mage or Fae—unless you knew what to look for, one would never spot most of these creatures in passing. On the other hand, people in the know didn't give it a passing thought to how obvious it was. This man was in that same category. I knew he was not, in fact, human.

"What's your name?" I asked, taking a pull of my beer. A few people had turned around to watch the game getting ready to unfold.

"Penance."

"That's a new one. I thought that was something you did."

"You're smarter than you look. It is. I don't think you could pronounce my real name."

The man opened the chess case, putting down the marble board. Pieces were placed as we both sat in silence. Admittedly, I had forgotten how to set up all the pieces. Penance blew out a huff of air and reached his long feathery fingers across the board to make some adjustments.

"Chess reminds me of life," the man started back up. For some reason, I wasn't really fazed by the oddness of it. "The moves you make in the beginning most definitely affect the ending."

"Well, you just reminded me I need another drink," I said, nodding over at Trish. We had drawn a small crowd around the table.

The lights were dim, the sounds of clinking glasses and low murmurs filling the air.

We looked at each other for a minute before Penance spoke up, "Are you sure you want to play?"

Looking around, I had a feeling the crowd wanted a show.

"Yup, let's do this," I said, giving him the go-ahead for the first move.

He struck out with his left knight, setting the tone for the rest of the match. For twenty minutes, we shuffled pieces while I chewed a light spot on my lip as I watched the cool, calculating player at the other end of the board.

"Checkmate," Penance purred in finality.

I stared at the board, sure I hadn't left an opening. There it was.

Jeers came from the crowd as the man's stare never faltered.

"Best two out of three?" I asked, sizing up the bet.

The man speculated for a minute. "Alright, tell you what. With game one, you owe me a favor. Payable in the next twenty-four hours. Game two is for the coins. I'll even pay you for the trouble of the favor," Penance said, the gold coin weighing heavy in my pocket.

I glanced over at Trish, seeing a neutral look on her face. She wasn't giving anything away tonight.

"Deal," I said as we reset the pieces.

I started this time, leading with my pawns, followed by my knights. The man did the same, mirroring my moves. I started getting frustrated as I counted down the final pieces.

He had me again. I pulled out the gold coin, smacking it on the table. Not too aggressively, but enough to make a point.

"Checkmate," the cool, calculating voice once again purred in finality.

"So, what's this favor?" I asked, figuring I had just gotten into something I probably would regret.

"Ah, the deed."

# CHAPTER 2

Ever realized you truly just messed something up? I stood in my room, looking down at my phone. A full day had passed since losing my bet with Penance. I was guessing that was a fake name, but nonetheless, I owed him a favor besides the coin Davros had given me.

The task was simple. Go to the Old City Cemetery in downtown Jacksonville and retrieve another coin from the tombstone of a soldier's wife simply named Agnes. The soldier also happened to once have been the mayor of Orlando, meaning that Agnes was once an important person. It was an old military tradition to leave coins on the tombstones of those you'd served with. Different denominations meant different types of military relationships. For tonight, I was to acquire a fifty-cent piece.

Penance had even offered to pay for my troubles if I was able to find the coin. He'd stated, "I'm not allowed on hallowed ground," whatever that meant. I knew it meant absolutely nothing with Vamps, so I was guessing he was just crazy. It all seemed like a bunch of bullshit, but I'd made a bet and knew better than to back out. Once retrieved, I would meet the obnoxiously good chess player back at FA's for a drink.

I had talked to Phil about the whole mess, him agreeing that the guy was crazy and that he would meet me at the cemetery if I needed him to. He was down for drinks later, though, no matter the outcome of my evening.

I decided to gate in from the Atheneum, as Riverplace Tower wasn't far from the cemetery, and there was a gate nearby. I kept thinking about Kim and her offer for dinner and drinks being pushed off another day.

The walk was a brisk ten-minute stroll. Since the Balance, people were more aware than before. In the past, walking through this part of Jacksonville Florida, would have garnered you a few mean stares. Now, people were more concerned with whether you would eat them or maybe turn them into a rat. Both just happened to be very rude and way too old-fashioned, even by Mage standards.

Arriving at the cemetery gates, a sinking feeling dropped in my stomach like a load of tacos after midnight. Something was hitting my senses on all cylinders. I hadn't felt this much energy since our trip to the South Pole, which had subsequently resulted in the destruction of a rather old geological feature. I had a reputation for that kind of stuff.

The night was humid. Moisture hung in the air as a light breeze ensured it stuck to you. The smell of grass, river water, and garbage from the city filled the air. Looking around, it was clear that the full moon was casting shadows at all angles. It was the perfect night for trouble.

I patted my blazer, ensuring I had all the necessary tools to protect myself. Durundle, my service pistol, and a few blended items, including an Evergate coin, were all in place. As always, the Evergate coin would bring me right back to the Postern and home. For a few minutes, I thought about going back to FA's to get more details from this guy, but figured it wouldn't matter.

There was trouble ahead, and I didn't have a clue what type.

There were a few large ornate grave markers I remembered seeing as a child. The one I was to go to tonight was made for someone named Agnes, the wife of a former captain and once mayor of Orlando. An angel was represented on the marker, and I was to check there first.

The coin had been left there by James, Agnes's husband, and to date, no one could or had removed it.

I walked up, not noticing the man sitting on the curb holding a small alligator.

The man let out a laughing cackle. "You sure you want to go in there, fella?" he asked in a scratchy, high-pitched tone.

I didn't have to get much closer to see he was more than likely a crackhead. Well, a crackhead with a pet alligator. I could lightly sense something coming from it.

I reached in my pocket, throwing the man a five. "Get something to eat. I'll be fine. Anything I need to know before I go in there?" I asked, figuring he had spent a good amount of his time in that spot.

"Are you afraid of ghosts?" the man cackled back, tucking the money in his pocket.

"I guess a little. Who isn't?" I said, taking in his question.

"Sounds like you're smart enough. You'll be fine," the man replied, standing up and holding the small alligator under his arm. "It's OK, Ralph. The dead man's not going to hurt you," the bum said, cooing at the animal before walking off.

I looked at the gate, the moonlighting the treetops. Walking around, I found a gap in the fence and squeezed through, grumbling about having to suck in way too much.

The scene inside the graveyard was textbook. A light fog covered the ground, making it hard to see your shoes. Shadows danced around the gravestones and trees, while the city's noise in the background contributed odd sounds that were hard to pick out.

The ground was crunchy underfoot, gravel with grass that hadn't been adequately maintained.

Unease settled in, convincing me to pull out Durundle. I could still see due to the moonlight, but for some reason, sounds were bouncing off everything. Echoes of voices, cars being driven, and metal clanking on concrete, filled the void.

I started focusing on one tree in particular. Scratching could be heard, loud, distinct, and absolutely coming from the tree. I walked, stubbing my toes on a few low headstones that had been worn down to nothing but small rocks.

“Shit,” I hissed, almost losing my footing, eyes laser-focused on the tree. No movement.

Within five feet of the tree, I could finally see what was causing the noise, making the hairs on my neck stand at full attention.

There, on the other side, was a rotted hand, the tip of a finger showing nothing but bone scraping the bark of the tree. It had dug a sizable hole in the trunk. The figure was covered in a dark, tattered robe, its face shielded from sight. Rasping came from the dark void.

“Ignis,” I whispered, pushing my will to the blade and springing it to life. Today, the sword had decided it would be a muted blood-red glow, not the flaming sword it was known to be. It had a mind of its own.

The creature didn’t flinch as the blade's red glow lit up what was once a face. Grated meat and bone flickered red as empty eye sockets stared at the tree, determined to keep digging.

The sound stopped. Holding my breath, I took two more steps to the side. It was like the thing didn’t know I was there.

I was wrong… the now animated creature lurched backward, pointing the sharpened finger it had been digging with at me. Jumping back, I pulled Durundle into the guard position above my head. The creature froze.

No longer in the shade of the tree, I could see the shimmer of moonlight passing through its apparitional body.

“Gods and graves, a ghost? You have to be shitting me,” I said, seeing my breath floating in the air, neither one of us moving, both sizing the other up.

For all intents and purposes, this was the first ghost I had run into. Sensing my distraction, the creature lurched again, swiping through the air with a violence to its speed and power that was very real.

If the bag of bones had landed that, I would've been in trouble. Still on my guard, I slashed down with my sword, cutting through the air. The whoosh of the blade sliced through the spirit and caught on what felt like meat and bones.

The ghost solidified under the smoldering of hellfire, now burning its cut-in-half body, fingers twitching as fabric disappeared. Looking closer, as the flame had cleared some of the fog, I could see both the creature and hellfire slowly winking out of existence.

Soon, I looked down to see no trace of either.

The familiar cackle of the disheveled old man with the alligator cut through the silence as I stood there, taking it in. "Looks like that one will not be coming back. The second death," the man said, chuffing. The alligator was now walking on a leash at his feet. The sound of him drinking a Slurpee echoed lightly as he hit the bottom of the cup.

"So, that was a ghost," I said, knowing from talking with Tom that they did exist. It's not that I doubted him. I just had never seen one before. "Second death?"

His alligator's tail was wagging like a dog's. "Hellfire is one of the few things that will do it. So, I'm guessing you're not exactly one of those normal magic types. You might just get what you came here for."

I was starting to think the man in front of me was putting on a show.

"What's that?" I asked, putting Durundle back in its sheath.

"The coin. Every once in a while, someone shows up looking for it. They can't even find it or see it. After what you just did, I'm pretty sure that part will be easy," the man replied, again taking a slurping drink through his straw and finalizing the last of his slushy.

"So there's a hard part?"

"Yup. Give me a couple more bucks. I want to go get a refill and watch."

I dropped five more dollars in his hand. The alligator hissed at me as the man giggled, walking off.

# CHAPTER 3

After a few minutes of reflecting and trying to figure if what had just happened had, in fact, just happened, the distant cackle of the odd man ground me back in reality.

"Where did he get that Slurpee?" I huffed, talking to the night air.

I pulled my short staff out, feeling its carvings under my fingers. I wasn't sure if killing ghosts was a good thing or not. I already had sleep issues.

Getting my bearings, I headed deeper into the cemetery, noticing more apparitions. Old headstones and unkempt ground crunched under my feet.

The old man with the alligator had stated they couldn't hit me "here," whatever that meant.

I looked over to see a woman sitting on a stone bench. The moonlight shimmering through her body let off a slight glow.

Unlike the creepy skeleton fingering the tree, she looked normal. Sad, but otherwise put together. Her dress reflected early to midcentury fashion. I was guessing the '20s.

I squatted down, getting eye level with her. She reminded me of Leshya. It was something about the eyes, or maybe the stare. Tom and I needed to have a chat about her at some point. It was due. After all, he was a necromancer, and what I was looking at resembled Leshya a little too much.

The figure slowly looked up at me. She had been crying for what I guessed was decades. The apparition looked straight through me before her eyes finally came into focus, showing confusion.

"Hey," I said in a low voice, seeing if it caught her attention.

The woman stared for a second before looking back down at the grave.

"Something there you need?"

She looked up at that, cocking her head. Like most people, I had watched enough ghost movies to know that usually got one's attention. Hell, after the Balance, the world had suddenly realized that most movies Hollywood pumped out were moderately instructional after-school specials.

The woman paused again, looking down at the grave. I took a minute to regain my bearings, figuring I would come back later and check it out. Maybe I'd even bring Tom, when he got back from wherever the hell he was.

As usual, not long after he showed up, he disappeared again.

I walked another fifty meters toward the large, carved grave marker. For some reason, more apparitions started showing up the closer I got to my target. I noticed a few taking a keen interest in my movements.

Checking my watch, I noticed Phil hadn't responded. The message was blue, so he had, in fact, gotten it before I left.

The large statue stuck out like a sore thumb even in the dark. It also appeared to have power pouring out of it, raising the hair on the back of my neck.

I looked down, shining the light of my phone on the name and confirming this was Agnes's grave. Inspecting the statue, I noticed the angel's hand was reaching down to what looked to be Agnes holding a child. No coin.

Coins were convenient vessels for enchantments and spells. The metal carrying the Etherium allowed it to be stored and used to the best of its abilities. I could feel power coming from the shrine, but again, no coin.

Looking closer at the statue, I noticed the angel's hand was smoother than the rest of the stone. It looked like years of people rubbing the hand for good luck, or whatever superstition this had tied to it.

Taking a deep breath and against my better judgment, I reached out and touched the hand of the angel, pushing my will into the statue.

A loud pop of ozone smacked the air as I fell back, the power from whatever it was I had just triggered flowing over my body like smoke. I stood up after a moment, feeling like I had just been sucked through multiple gates at once: slightly drained and disoriented.

Once up, it was clear that, while I was still in the graveyard, I was absolutely on a different Plane.

Apparitional shapes, now solid, started moving, noise coming from their sudden unease. I had a strong feeling that they were not so harmless anymore.

Sounds started filling the once silent night. A constant grinding rumble reverberated in the background. It wasn't the familiar sounds of the city, and at that moment, I realized I wasn't in Kansas—well, Florida—anymore. At least, not the one I knew.

Patting my blazer, I checked that Durundle and my short staff were still there. The hilt brought comfort to my otherwise freaking out mind.

A pirate—I was guessing "pirate" due to his clothes—stood approximately ten feet away. The long, flowing black beard made the scowl on his face more intense and threatening.

He of course, upon further inspection, had a peg leg and an exceptionally large saber in hand.

The look on his face was one of calculation; he had yet to figure out what I was. I was the new fish in the tank, and the pirate was the shark. As I guessed any good pirate would, he decided to attack first and ask questions later.

His saber whistled down. Instinctively, almost as if on cruise control, I pulled Durundle from its sheath, filling the night with glittering red hellfire.

When the sword decided to go into this mode, it made the surrounding area look as if someone had dropped a red flare.

For those not aware, the sword had a mind of its own at times. Moving and pushing me in ways I normally wouldn't be able to accomplish.

The one thing about a trained swordsman or woman was that they had usually done it all their life. I was new to the sword game, and on top of that, my attacker had what looked to be a few centuries of practice.

In most cases, years of experience was the reason Mages were so skillful at using hand-to-hand combat weapons. Decades of practice left even professionals at the top of their game outclassed when compared to Mages. Mages and Ethereals alike often didn't even enchant their weapons as they were, in fact, that good.

I was not at that level yet, so Durundle again came to life, taking on a mind of its own and driving my hands to work on a level I had yet to earn. Hey, if you're not cheating, you're not trying.

The hissing blade swung down, slamming into the saber. It was the first time the sword hadn't eaten through whatever it touched. We both pulled back, reassessing. The large bearded man lunged again, leaving his lower body and peg leg open.

Swinging again, I missed his blade on purpose, instead aiming for the odd-looking wooden leg. The effect was fast and final as the man fell to the ground. A bellow of frustration came from his throat, death shooting from his eyes.

I had attacked not only him but his pride. My thinking behind that was not to kill any more ghosts, sending them to their final death—or under my bed at night.

Walking closer, I saw what I was looking for: a coin just like the one I had hanging off his neck on a chain that fell out when he hit the ground.

We looked at each other as he started crawling toward his saber. A flaming arrow whistled through the air, hissing as it passed my head and cut my cheek. I crouched, looking around.

No origin. The pirate, knowing its invisible source, did as any pirate would and started cussing.

"Hornswoggling, ass jack!" the bearded man on the ground exclaimed in a rough, bellowing voice, his accent not placeable but there. He was not happy with the arrow, directing his curses toward the new attacker.

Great, more issues, I thought, darting around the statue and touching it again in hopes of leaving. Nothing. Another arrow slammed into the statue from behind. Either the attacker was lightning fast or there was more than one.

Other figures, once looming, also dove for cover. I think I triggered the security system, whatever that is in an old graveyard in another Plane.

Another flaming arrow forced me to my feet and on the move. I ran back in the direction I had come, maneuvering around trees as the arrows slowed down. The shuffling of feet away from the statue filled the air. Whatever was throwing the flaming arrows had everything else in the cemetery going for cover.

I looked to the right, seeing the sad woman's familiar outline, now solid, still sitting on the bench. This time, she was pushing a hand into the ground with her feet as she wept. The scene was surreal.

Letting out a light whistle, her strained look of concentration broke for a moment as she looked up. She motioned with her head for me to come over. The look was pleading.

I wasn't sure if my second attacker was bound to a particular area, but decided to take my chances, slowly creeping out from behind the tree.

"Please," the woman said in a breathless voice that had been holding in that very word for decades.

The hand was gnarled, its familiar, pointed fingers sticking up razor-sharp. Grayish skin stretched to the point of eruption on its knuckles.

It was the hand of a vampire. The issue was, here, I couldn't figure out if it was dead, alive, or somewhere in between.

The hand looked apparitional, not solid like the other figures, telling me that it was very real in the world I had just come from. It appeared the woman was trying to keep it from crossing over. Things here were the opposite.

She looked at the sword in my hand. I had let the flames out when I'd gone on the move, seeking concealment.

A flaming sword was probably the most conspicuous thing one could have.

"You want me to," I asked in the form of a statement, referring to driving the blade through the ground into whatever lay beneath.

The woman started shaking as her mouth slowly started moving. She was pretty in an eerie manner, like Leshya.

"Cannot leave. He can't leave," she said in a strained, hushed voice.

I looked back, seeing movement in the shadows but no more arrows.

"Why?" I asked, the look of frustration growing on her face.

"Spread pain, death, sadness," she said, her calm voice growing slightly louder. The hand was becoming more animated as she spoke, reacting to her voice.

In reality, I was not sure what the repercussions of killing something in this Plane could possibly be. I wasn't under immediate threat. The woman obviously was.

I couldn't do it. Noise again filled the air, bringing my senses back into focus as the ground under the hand started moving.

A quick snap of wood echoed as the hand reached toward the foot the woman was using to push the vampire down. A moment later, the other hand erupted, grabbing the woman firmly by the ankle.

She gasped as fear crossed her face. "OK, now we have an issue, buddy," I said, igniting Durundle sweeping down on both hands, sending them flying through the air.

The woman gasped, her eyes going wild. She knew death awaited her at those hands.

I swung the sword overhead, holding it upside down as I decided the location to land the hit. Taking a breath, I thrust down the center of the now gone hands. The sword plunged into the damp earth with no resistance, the flaming blade hissing as it pushed further into the ground.

The two stumps spasmed then fell still.

I looked over to the woman wearing a nervous smile. Not out of happiness, but out of mercy, and regret. You know, the smile you saw at a funeral when someone was remembering better days long since past.

She reached toward me as her solid body faded away into mist.

The roar of an engine, followed by two beaming headlights, flooded the cemetery. Figures shuffled out of sight. In the far distance, two long-dead soldiers stared blankly into the light.

There was something unearthly about the entire situation. The sky above had an odd purple hue to it, and the light odor of wet, stale soil filled the air.

As if reading my mind, the black-bearded pirate turned to see the headlights, his eyes gleaming in the sparkling illumination.

The angry pirate was dragging himself toward the monument and grave marker for Agnes... I caught his eyes, looking up at the trees before turning back to the task at hand.

Getting to the monument first.

My stomach dropped, thinking of the repercussions. I wasn't an old wise mage, but I knew that the coin on his sash was, in fact, a gate coin, and the monument was some type of gate. I was betting that if he made it to the monument, I would be stuck.

We both refocused at the same time. I pulled out my service pistol and slammed Durundle into its sheath, the blade disappearing into the enchanted hilt and dissolving its size.

Phil had taught me a thing or two, mainly that I was better off carrying "loaded" ammunition explicitly made to handle Ethereals and Mages.

Taking off at a sprint, it was clear that whatever was slinging arrows or driving the vehicle didn't have the same agenda. Arrows flew overhead, precise and rhythmic. One arrow landed close to my feet, the person behind the flaming bolts letting me know I was next.

The sound of broken glass filled the air as I finally caught up with the bearded man. He had turned and was pointing his saber at me. A look of determined hate, covering his face.

I politely pulled up my pistol, pointing it at his face. Again, the sound of an engine revving filled the air, the lights shifting as the arrow-shooting part of the party kept firing at the vehicle.

"So, two options," I said to the pirate, feeling a light hammering on my chest.

"Looks like you have other problems, scallywag," the man said in a deep, rumbling voice.

"No, we have a problem. I saw the arrows skinning your ass as well," I said in a rush, knowing time was ticking.

"Give me the coin, and we will call it even."

"What if I don't," the man said in serious reflection. He was not as ignorant as he looked.

"Then we have a problem that will not end in your favor."

The man let out a laugh, as the sound of a vehicle crashing

into a rock filled the air. Whatever had happened with the other things in the cemetery was over.

"Here. Before you leave, know that everything you take has a price to it. I'm not giving this to you freely."

Motioning for him to throw the coin, he tossed it at my feet in a sash. He hadn't looked at the pistol once, telling me he didn't see it as a threat. I'd spotted an old flintlock pistol in his waistband earlier.

Something wasn't adding up with the man either way. I wondered for a slight second if he was like me, stuck on this Plane.

The first arrow slammed into the man's shoulder. He didn't move. A smile crossed his face as he pulled out his pistol. I started to squeeze the trigger, and the flintlock pistol roared to life. The round screamed by my ear, filling it with the familiar buzzing ping I had grown to know in the army.

The shot had staggered me, slightly blurring my vision.

The man laughed again, the sound muffled. His mouth was full of black and gold teeth. He started cackling, looking over my shoulder.

The sound of flesh crashing to earth filled the ringing silence. Again, the man laughed. Whatever had shot the arrows at us was no longer a threat. He'd pulled the pistol and shot before I could react. The pirate could have killed me at any time.

Done playing games, I picked up the sash holding the coin in my hand. Power radiated from the piece, flooding my senses.

I pulled the coin out of the cloth and held it to the hand in the monument, willing to leave.

The sounds of laughter filled the air as the familiar pull of a gate dragging me back to reality filled my body.

Unlike with normal gating, I was, needless to say, not really in my body at the time of landing. My body jerked as a hammer-crushing blow fell on my chest.

My eyes snapped open as I gasped for air, finding my nose

was blocked.

There, hovering over me, was Phil, about to perform mouth-to-mouth resuscitation. The hammering blows on my chest had obviously been chest compressions.

I raised my knee, fully extending my leg and pushing Phil back enough to evade the angry, bearded Irish hipster about to violate my personal space.

"You're alive," Phil bellowed, clenching his fists and raising them to the sky.

I sat there, tasting the familiar tang of tobacco. I think he got a few breaths in. The issue was, I wasn't dead. I'd made my way back.

Looking up and seeing the excitement on Phil's face, I decided to let the moment carry on. He, of course, continued.

"I'll never have to buy my own drinks again. You see that," Phil said, pointing over to the homeless man standing there drinking another Slurpee.

Oddly enough, he was no longer walking his pet alligator. It had been replaced by a thick man with a longer than average neck, wearing a green suit and eating a tin of open sardines. Just when I thought things couldn't get any stranger, they did...

"Ya, I owe you one," I said, standing up and dusting myself off. "What's going on here?"

"Bruther, all hell. I show up. This guy's drinking a Slurpee with this, well, thing. Next thing I know, I'm running through the cemetery, and a pair of damn vampire hands go flying through the air like whoosh." Phil was good at making sound effects when he was excited.

"Then, I find you lying here stone-cold dead, and then I do my little medical thing, and here you are!" Phil finally concluded, lighting up a smoke.

The sound of jaws slapping coming from the man in the green suit caught our attention as he lifted the tin of sardines to his mouth, eating the entire thing, metal and all.

"Who's your friend?" I asked, looking into the reptilian eyes of the now humanoid figure.

"Al. You've already met," the man said, taking a finishing pull from the straw for the second time. I was guessing the now standing alligator had gone from Ralph to Al.

"Fair enough. I think I need a drink," I said, figuring that I had just met my first true shifter.

"Did you get what you were looking for?" the man asked as Al cracked his neck, moving it in a circular motion.

"Ya, you could say that."

"Let me give you some advice,"

Phil interrupted. "Hang on. Do we have a problem?"

"No problem, I can assure you. My companion and I are perfectly fine. Whatever it is you found, take it far from here and never bring it back. Many people have come here looking for it. Most never get up off the ground," the man said, coughing at the group without covering his mouth.

"What's he on about?" Phil asked, cocking his head while still grinning. "Oh, I called Frank to handle the vampire hand thing. Was that you?"

I shook my head, taking the last five-dollar bill out of my pocket before handing it to the man. "Here, the next one's on me," I said as a grin spread across his face.

The two turned, walking off into the fog.

# CHAPTER 4

We both got in the car after Phil gave me two more accounts of him saving my life. "Tell you what, you've earned it. Let's hop over to FA's for a drink. I'm going to call this whack job and get this mess behind me," I said under my breath.

After a full accounting of events to Phil, I realized he had pulled over and was staring at me.

"What?"

"Bruther, I think you were in the Perdition."

"Perdition?"

"You know, Purgatory, the in-between, whatever the hell else you call it. I've never seen a real ghost, and you just strolled down to the halfway house to hell and picked a fight. I'm not sure about this one; the car saving you, the vampire, the pirate... We need to talk to Tom or check you into rehab."

"About that, any word on where he is?" I asked, both chuffing at his joke. Phil, looking concerned, pulled back out onto A1A.

"On some mission. Won't be back for a few weeks."

I needed to talk to Gramps, or as I now called him since his remarkable rising from the dead, Tom. He was, after all, a Necromancer.

Since we now conveniently lived next door to FA's, I took a

few minutes to get cleaned up and text the number the guy had left me. I didn't think people really called anyone anymore.

After a few minutes and a quick change of clothes, I received a text letting me know he was there.

This text was followed by a picture of Petro and Casey on their honeymoon. In typical Petro fashion, he was wearing a Speedo while standing by a pool.

There was something about seeing an eight-inch-tall, mustached pixie in a Speedo that made me turn off the screen.

Phil and I talked before going into FA's. He was to carry an e-meter in his pocket to see if he could get a reading off the guy. The meter was handy in figuring out what type of person or thing someone was.

We weren't expecting trouble, especially not with Trish and Amon running the bar. Still, something about the entire episode seemed manufactured, like a setup, and I, as always, wanted to know more.

We walked through the door with our usual nod to Trish. The place was packed full for a Friday night, and the only open spaces were at the knee wall separating the dining and table area from the large bar. The smell of copper, cooking steak, and light smoke filled the air.

Trish had hired a few more people to work the bar and was the first to walk up, handing us our drinks without taking our order. As always, she was right.

"Let me guess. The weird guy in the hood standing at the jukebox playing Whitney Houston songs on repeat?" Trish asked me, already knowing.

"Yup. I want to figure out why he sent me to a haunted graveyard."

"I need to hear this one sometime. No trouble, Max, I mean it," Trish said before walking back to the bar.

We shuffled over to the jukebox after a few reflective pulls of our drinks.

The man was staring transfixed at the machine. It was as if he had never heard this type of music before.

"Hey, I'm here to balance the scales," I said, a term used in the magical community to settle a bet or favor, tapping the man on the shoulder.

The man lowered the hood of his cape, turning around with a slight grin on his face.

"The music is amazing, gentlemen," Penance said, reaching out to shake only my hand.

Phil smirked.

"Let us go take a seat. I will get us another round of drinks. If you have indeed been successful, we have much to celebrate."

We walked over to a corner table, pushing through a loud group of Vs out for a night of fun away from the regulars.

Since the Balance, some things had changed. For starters, FA's had become slightly busier due to folks in the magical community wanting to escape somewhere they could—literally, in some cases—let their hair down.

Thanks to recent books and love-story movies, Vampires had drawn a good amount of the regular population's attention. It seemed they still had trouble understanding that being bitten by a V—unless you were a Fae—would not turn you into a sparkly, eternal vampire. Not to mention most Vs were annoyingly protective of regulars.

There had been a few pop-up specialty restaurants and vampire-themed bars open. These folks avoided them like the plague. If you met someone claiming to be V at one of those places, they had been paid to be there, or you were more than likely being catfished. There were still bad ones out there. They just didn't hang out at bars that sold Vampire Lover T-shirts.

"Let's see it," Penance said, licking his upper lip, eyes gleaming. Phil had a hand in his pocket, obviously trying to get a reading on the e-meter.

I pulled out the coin, wrapped in a napkin, letting it clunk on the table. It spun on its side, making a whirling metallic sound on the bartop, catching the man's attention.

Before the man could pick it up, I slammed my hand down on top of it, gaining some looks of interest from the crowd.

"Not so fast. I was about killed getting this simple task—as you put it—completed. What's so special about this gate coin?" I asked, seeing the frustration in his eyes. I could also notice Trish peering over as I shook my head.

"Gate coin? It's not a gate coin; rather, a key. A key to a special place. It was stolen from me."

It took me a minute to digest what he'd said, taking another pull of my beer. He was telling the truth. At least, as much of it as he wanted.

"So, let me guess. The pirate stole it from you to do what?"

"You met Blackbeard. I was wondering if he was still alive."

"Alive? You mean he wasn't one of those apparitions?"

"Oh, he's very much alive if you saw him, or he would be in the under. What happened to him?"

Figuring I'd hold some cards to my chest, I answered in my best "holding facts back" manner. "I don't truly know."

The man reflected on my statement. "Fine, and your friend there has already let you in on where you were. This key is dangerous and needs to get back to its proper resting place."

I still didn't trust him as I finally lifted my hand, scooting the coin over.

"Thank you. Oh, and for your troubles." Penance reached into his pocket, handing me back the coin I'd lost earlier and the silver one.

"Do make sure you don't spend these in the same place. I would hang on to them for sentimental value."

Great, another riddle. The man stood up as Trish walked

over.

"Excuse me. I'm letting you know you are not welcome back here," Trish ordered with complete authority.

The man thinly smiled. "I wasn't planning on it. Good night," Penance said, pulling the cloak back over his head before walking out.

Trish watched with sharp eyes as the man walked through the crowd, leaving. As the door closed behind him, Trish turned to look at us. Three beers had mysteriously appeared in her hands as she sat down.

I again retold the events of the past couple of days, handing Trish the coins.

"These feel off," she announced, placing them back on the table. "When you brought the first one in, I could feel the power coming off it. Now that they're together, it's changed."

"I'm getting the same thing. My gut's telling me this whole thing was on purpose. Like on rails or something. Either way, I'll put these up and dig into them more later."

The three of us agreed, finishing our beers.

Phil pulled out the e-meter. The device was the size of a large cell phone and picked up specific traces of Ethereum. In turn, it would then supply a few readings to help determine how long the traces had been present—not useful here—and the type of Mage/ Ethereal or lack thereof.

The meter gave a neutral reading, much like the one it gave when used on me.

We all looked at each other.

"I'm pretty sure he's not a demon," I said, grinning slightly. After all, I was a quarter demon, and had a good feel for the type.

Trish leaned forward to gain more privacy. "I think he may have been one of the Old Gods, or an Ethereal deity of some type."

"Can you translate that, lass," Phil said, rolling an unlit cigarette in his mouth.

"A messenger from the gods, here for a reason," Trish clarified, making ghost noises as she stood up, lightening the mood. "Good night, boys."

We said our goodnights, walking the few steps needed to the apartment. I had talked to Phil about moving in, however, he still insisted on staying at the Atheneum.

"Are you stopping by tomorrow?" I asked as Phil activated the gate.

"Wouldn't miss it for the world, bruther," he responded, saluting me as he walked through the gate.

I was alone in the apartment slash new offices of Abaddon & Associates, which just happened to be having its grand opening in the morning.

Walking upstairs and opening the nightstand drawer, I deposited the two coins wrapped in a napkin.

That night, I dreamt of pirates and ghoulish, disembodied vampire hands chasing me around the beer aisle at Publix.

# EPILOGUE

Abaddon & Associates (AA)
Consulting commercial and private. Questions answered.
Re-birthday testing. Council-certified Castor dealer.
See a Consultant for rates

# JUSTIN S. LESLIE BIO

Justin is a retired, highly decorated army major who completed several tours in Afghanistan. He startedwriting after his misadventures landed him back in the real world and everyday life. This outlet has allowed Justin to indulge in often-needed escapes from the rat race.

Justin has focused on building his own magical worlds to share with readers, as well as enjoying ones created by fellow authors. He is, in fact, a huge book nerd…

He also holds an MBA from the University of Maryland with a Bachelors from Maryville College, and currently runs a national sales program for one of those big mega-companies.

When he isn't writing, playing music, or spending time with his wife and two boys, he can be found in his Doctors Inlet home, immersed in the latest urban fantasy, or a well-made old fashioned. His inspiration has come from all the other authors in the genre who've helped him through endless tough hours needing to take a break.

*Note from author*: Yes, I didn't write all that cheesy stuff above…maybe just some of it.

To all my brothers and sisters in the armed forces, cheers, and may the wind be forever at your back. To those we've lost along the way, you will be forever missed.

"Halfway down the trail to Hell in a shady meadow green,"

www.justinleslie.com
Facebook—Justin Leslie
Buy Max Abaddon and the Will Book 1
Buy Max Abaddon and the Purity Law Book 2

www.ingramcontent.com/pod-product-compliance
Lightning Source LLC
LaVergne TN
LVHW050947080826
845145LV00004B/1450

* 9 7 8 1 7 3 5 3 0 3 5 7 4 *